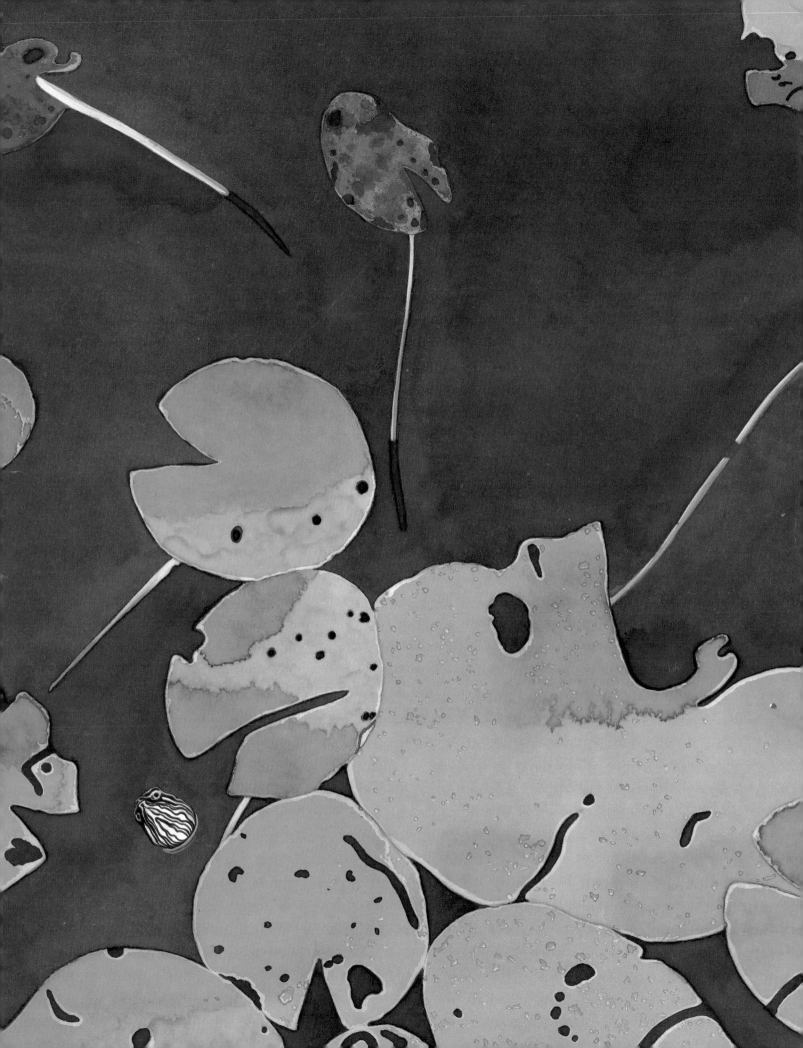

LINDSAY BARRETT GEORGE

Around the Pond: Who's Been Here?

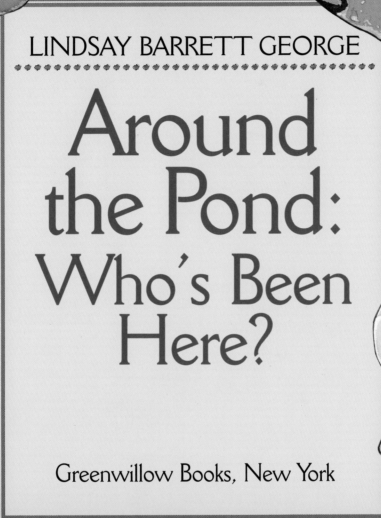

Greenwillow Books, New York

It is warm and muggy on this summer afternoon.

"Cammy," says William, "Mom says if we pick enough blueberries, we can make a pie for dinner."

"Let's go!" says Cammy.

Cammy and her brother grab their berry containers and follow the old deer path that circles the pond.

A dead sugar maple stands alone by the water's edge.

White feathers are stuck to the bark around a hole.

Who's been here?

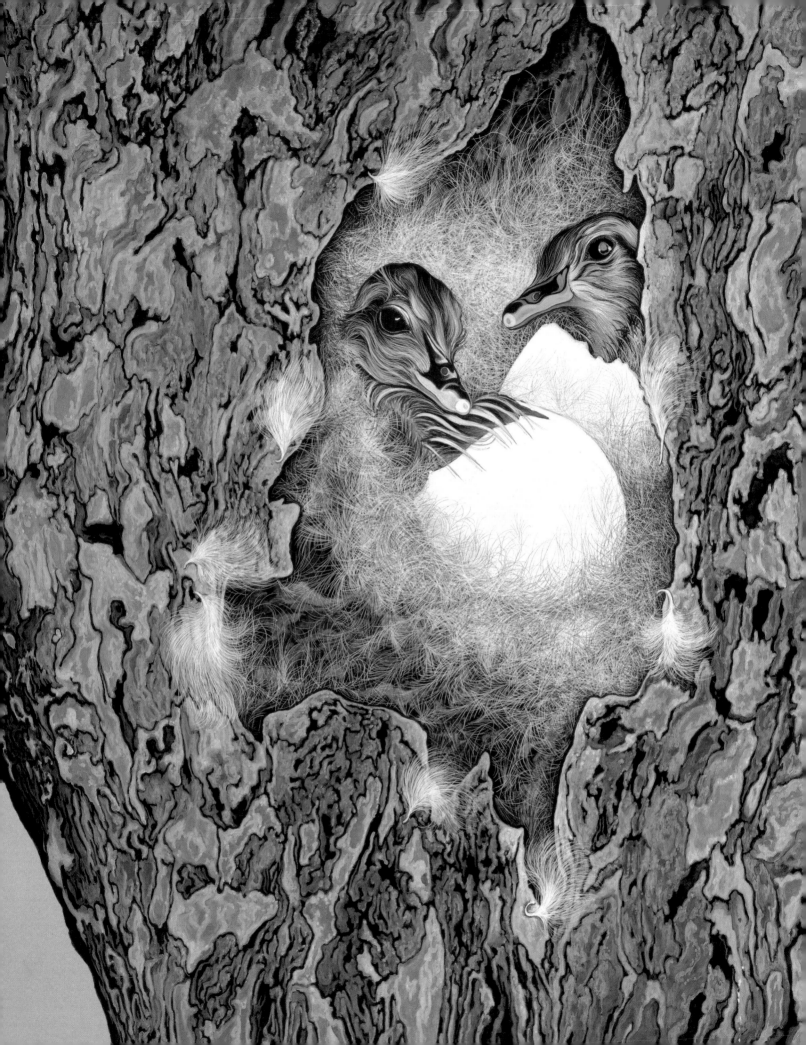

Two baby
wood ducks.

Sam finds a stick.

He wants someone to throw it.

"Not now, Sam," William says.

"We've got to pick blueberries."

Their dog lies down on the soft
sphagnum moss.

"William, look at this footprint,"
says Cammy.

Who's been here?

A baby raccoon.

A tree has fallen across the path and into the pond.
William dangles his feet in the water.
He sees a shallow crater on the sandy bottom.

Who's been here?

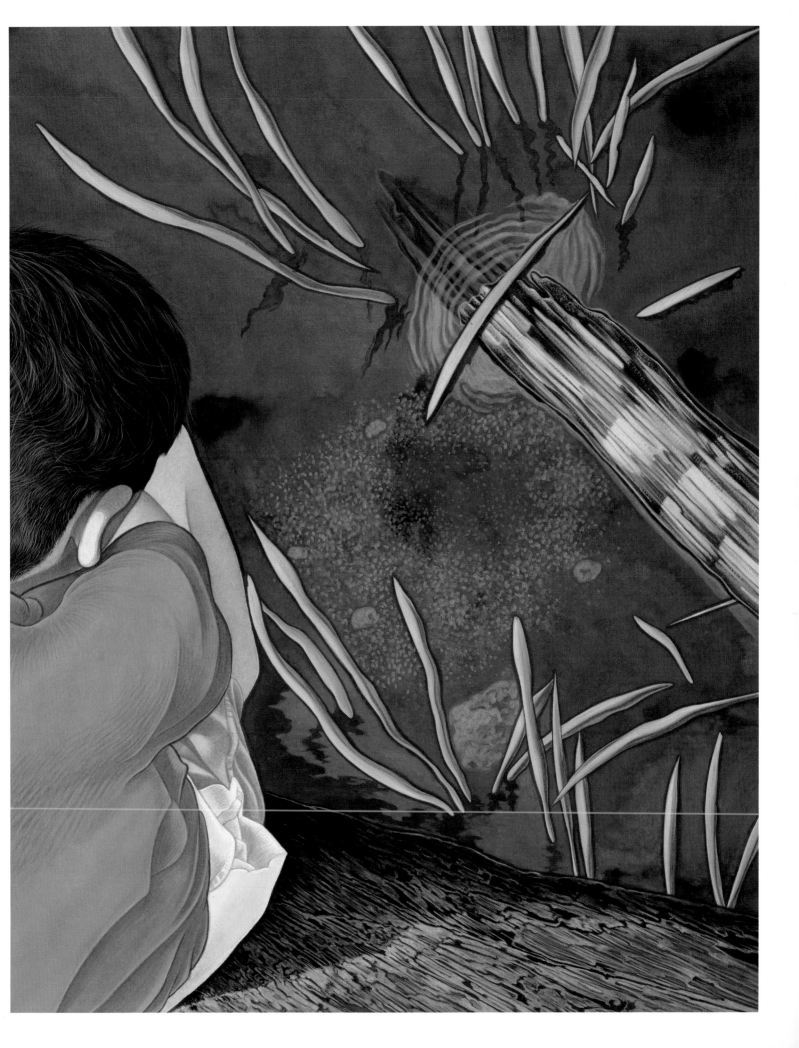

A sunfish.

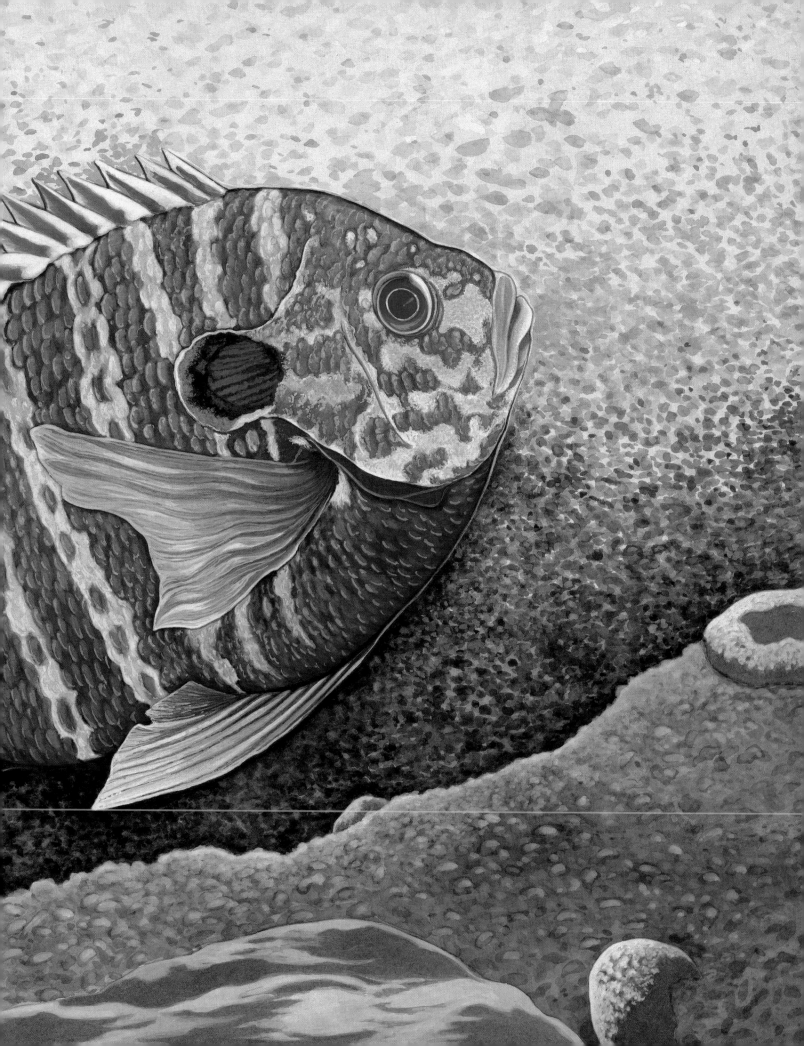

Cammy and William reach a patch of swamp azalea.

They see a pile of branches and mud.

Who's been here?

A beaver.

Bits of broken shell lie on the sunny bank.

The children stop to take a closer look.

William picks up a piece of shell.

It is soft.

Who's been here?

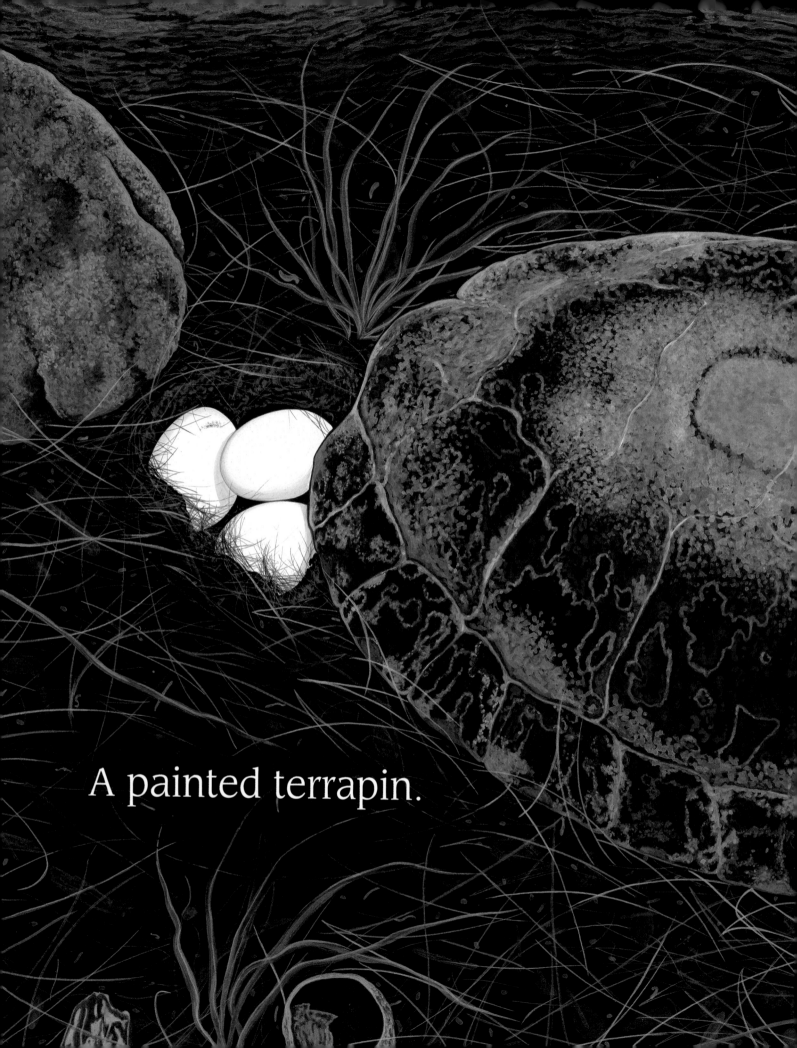

A painted terrapin.

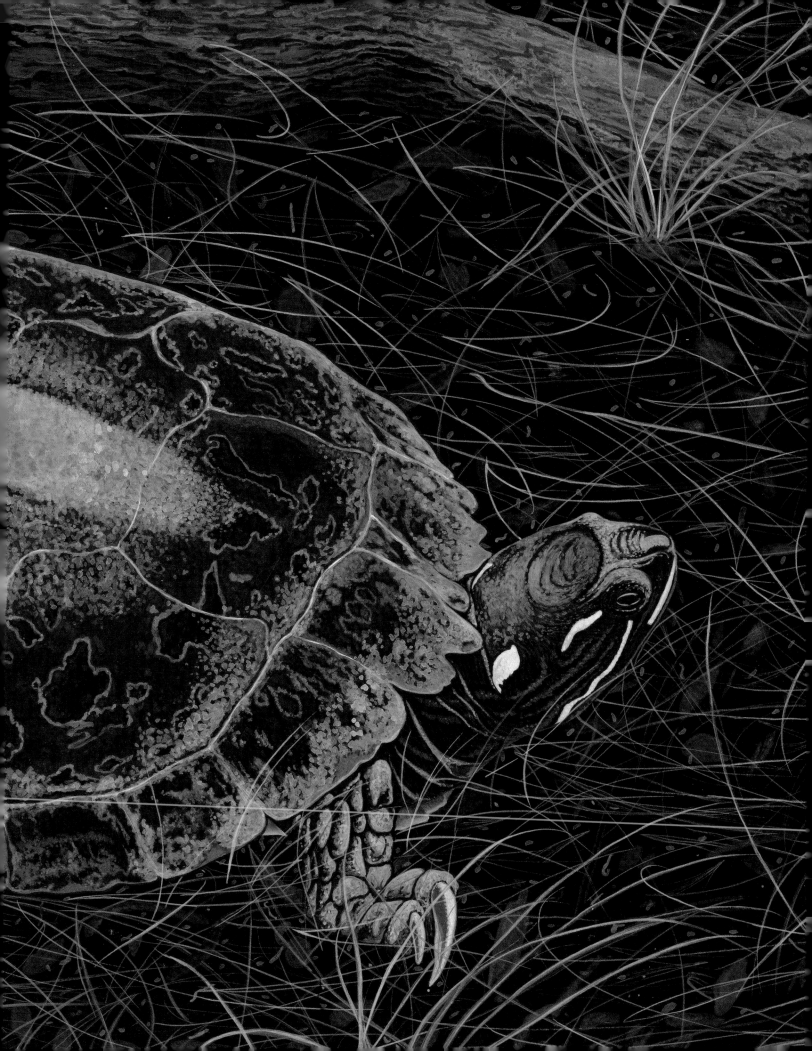

Cammy and her brother stop in front
of a large blueberry bush.
They pick and eat.
Sam likes blueberries, too.
Cammy points to a long, filmy shape
caught on the branches.

Who's been here?

A garter snake.

Sam wades into the pond and takes a drink.

A red-winged blackbird scolds from a nearby branch.

A large, gray feather floats next to a lily pad.

Who's been here?

A great blue
heron.

The pond is quiet and still.
The late afternoon sky turns pink.
"Let's go wading," says Cammy.
The mud is soft and squishy.
"Look at all the mussel shells," says
William.

Who's been here?

An otter.

Cammy and William reach the dock.
They have eaten most of their blueberries.
But look! Two full pails of berries are
waiting for them.

Who's been here?
They know!

"Come and join us,"
calls their father.
And in they go!

A mother **wood duck** laid its eggs in the hollow of a tree and tucked feathers and down around them to keep them warm. These newly hatched ducklings will stay in the nest for about a day. Then they will leap to the ground, and the parent ducks will show them how to find nuts, insects, and plants to eat.

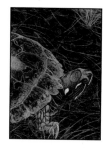

In summer the female **painted terrapin** digs a hole in sandy ground near the water's edge. There it lays a clutch of three to fifteen eggs, which will hatch within three months. The baby turtles scurry to the water soon after they hatch. Terrapins love to sunbathe on rocks and logs in ponds, lakes, or streams.

A baby **raccoon** looks for food around the pond's edge. Raccoons live in shrubby areas near water and are active at night. They use their front paws to search for food, reaching under stones and feeling in shallow water for crayfish, nymphs, mussels, frogs, and fish. Raccoons also like to eat nuts and berries.

The **garter snake** is the most common species of snake in North America. It lives near water and may grow to as much as three feet in length. Several times a year a snake "sheds its skin" by rubbing against rough objects until the thin outer layer of dead skin slips off its body.

A male **sunfish** makes a nest in shallow water along the shore. Using its tail, the male brushes a saucer-shaped depression in the sandy bottom. If a female sunfish likes the nest, it will lay its eggs there. The male will fertilize the eggs and then guard the nest from other fish.

The **great blue heron** is a large, graceful bird that stalks fish, frogs, small snakes, and salamanders in shallow water. The heron is not really blue, but gray. When it stands motionless in water, it looks like a sun-bleached tree stump—until it strikes at its prey with its long, sharp bill.

This **beaver** is bringing a branch to its house in the pond, called a lodge. The lodge is made of wood, mud, and stones, and the branch will be used to patch a leak in the walls. A beaver spends most of its waking time looking for food (plants and the bark of trees), maintaining its lodge and dam, and rearing its young.

The **river otter** is a very playful animal that lives both on land and in water. It may build a den in a riverbank, but often it will take over an old beaver lodge or muskrat den. Otters like to eat mussels, fish, snakes, birds' eggs, and young birds.

For John and Clare, with gratitude

Special thanks to Matt George, Jon Lowris from Pocono Snake and Animal Farm, Jennifer Mattive from T & D's Mountain Road Menagerie, Wallenpaupack North Intermediate School, Judy Weiss, and my family

Library of Congress Cataloging-in-Publication Data
George, Lindsay Barrett. Around the pond : who's been here? / by Lindsay Barrett George.   p.   cm.   Summary: While picking blueberries on a warm summer afternoon, Cammy and her brother see signs of unseen animals and their activities including footprints, a dam, and a floating feather.   ISBN 0-688-14376-8 (trade).   ISBN 0-688-14377-6 (lib. bdg.)
[1. Animals—Habits and behavior—Fiction.   2. Summer—Fiction.]   I. Title.   PZ7.G29334Ar   1996   [E]—dc20   95-25080   CIP   AC